The Eagle and the Rainbow

The Eagle and the Rainbow

Timeless Tales from México

Antonio Hernández Madrigal
illustrated by Tomie dePaola

FULCRUM
GOLDEN, COLORADO

For My Parents

Antonio   1923–1995
Maria Refugio   1926–1995

*I dedicate this book to share
the dream that has come true.*

First paperback edition 2009
Text © 1997 Antonio Hernández Madrigal
Original illustrations (by special arrangement with G. P. Putnam's Sons) © 1997 Tomie dePaola

Library of Congress Cataloging-in-Publication Data

Madrigal, Antonio Hernández.
    The eagle and the rainbow : timeless tales from Mexico / Antonio Hernandez Madrigal ; illustrated by Tomie dePaola.
        p.   cm.
    Contents: The eagle and the rainbow (Huichol legend) — Tahui (Tarahumara legend) — The boy who cried tears of jade (Mayan legend) — The deer tribe (Tarascan legend) — Legend of the feathered serpent (Aztec legend)
    ISBN 978-1-55591-317-5 (hardcover)
    ISBN 978-1-55591-728-9 (paperback)
    1. Indians of Mexico—Folklore. 2. Tales—Mexico. [1. Indians of Mexico—Folklore. 2. Folklore—Mexico.] I. dePaola, Tomie, ill. II. Title.
    F1219.3.F6M34   1997
    398.2 '0972—dc21   —dc21
    [[398.2]]   96-46159
                                                                                CIP
                                                                                AC

Book design by Alyssa Pumphrey

Printed in China
0 9 8 7 6 5 4 3 2 1

Fulcrum Publishing
4690 Table Mountain Drive, Suite 100
Golden, Colorado 80403
800-992-2908 • 303-277-1623
www.fulcrumbooks.com

Contents

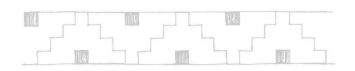

The Eagle and the Rainbow

The Eagle and the Rainbow

A Huichol Legend

Long before the time of the ancestors, when Earth was young, the desert spirits met in the sacred land of Wiricuta. "Of what use to the earth are the cactus and its fruit, which I have created?" grumbled the Spirit of the Plants.

"And the water springs I have created?" added Mother Rain.

"There is no one to breathe the air that blows across the sky," Father Wind complained. The desert land was an empty and lonely place, so the spirits agreed upon creating the Huichols, the people at the center of the earth.

The spirits were pleased as the people breathed the air, drank the water, and ate the cactus and its fruit. From among the people they chose a man to become the *Mara'kame,* or holy man. The Mara'kame would lead the others into the ways of the spirits.

When the fifth child was born, he was brought by his parents, Yumari and his wife, Aríma, to the Mara'kame.

"Great Mara'kame, please find a name for our child," they asked. According to the ways revealed by the spirits, it was the Mara'kame's duty to find in his dreams a name for each newborn.

"I shall search for his name every night," he responded. The spirits in time would come and help him find a name. He also knew that this fifth child would bear a special fate, for he was born under the sacred number of the Huichol.

When darkness came, the Mara'kame prayed to the spirits, asking that a name for the child be revealed to him. On the third night a vision came to his dreams. While he held the fifth child in his arms, the Mara'kame saw that they had arrived at the center of the earth. When he looked upward, he spotted the sacred eagle flying in a circle above the two of them. As he raised the newborn, one of its feathers landed upon the child's forehead. In the morning when the Mara'kame awoke, he called upon the people. "The sacred eagle will share its name with the fifth child," he said.

The men and women became displeased at hearing his words, as none of their children had been given a name that belonged to the spirits. "No mortal is worthy of carrying the sacred eagle's name!" the crowd protested.

"You must find another name for this child," they demanded.

The Mara'kame once again searched his dreams. For many moons he prayed to the spirits to help him find a different name for the fifth child. He also asked for the help of the desert lords. But no other vision ever came to him. The child was thus destined to live without a name. And for as long as he bore no name, his soul would be in great danger and at the mercy of the evil spirits.

As time passed the fifth child became known as Fast as Deer, for his legs were faster than any other boy's. He also showed a courage and strength far above the others. Fast as Deer climbed the highest hills and collected the largest and tastiest eggs of wild birds. He also gathered the ripest fruits from the tallest cactus. Each night once Takauyasi, or Father Sun, had walked across the skies and darkness came upon the desert land, Fast as Deer returned with more squirrels and rabbits than all the others.

"Ah! I wish this young man lived in my hut," his parents overheard other men and women whispering when he returned from the hunt.

But one day, when the first people became old, Mother Rain did not appear. They soon grew worried as Father Sun blew his hot breath over the desert land like scalding fire. The water springs soon dried out, and the cactus slowly began to die. The squirrels and rabbits also fled to other lands in search of food and water. Hunger and thirst came over the Huichols as the life-giving rain did not come. "Mother Rain must be displeased with us," the people told one another.

"We must ask the great Mara'kame for his help," all agreed, and so they went to him.

"Great Mara'kame, you who speak the language of the spirits, ask Mother Rain to have mercy upon us," they begged.

The Mara'kame went into his hut and returned wearing his ceremonial clothes. "You must awaken the spirits with your tepus," he ordered. The men soon alerted the spirits by beating their *tepus,* or three-legged drums. Meanwhile the Mara'kame prayed facing south, the desert corner where the deities dwelled. For many days he aimed toward the sky his *urus,* the arrows adorned with the sacred eagle feathers. He also prayed in the holy language. But his pleas were not answered.

"The desert spirits are greatly displeased with us," he explained to the people.

"How else can we beg their forgiveness?" an elder asked him. But the Mara'kame did not know how to respond.

Each night the Mara'kame searched for the answer in his dreams. One morning he again spoke to the people. "You and your children must dance to the spirits and pray that they bring an end to the drought," the Mara'kame instructed.

Soon the young and old, the weak and strong, wore their ceremonial clothing adorned with beads and feathers. Facing toward the sacred land of Wiricuta, they chanted and prayed from dawn until dusk, according to the instructions of the Mara'kame. But their humble voices were still not heard and everyone began to grow discouraged and weak. After many days had passed, the Mara'kame said in defeat, "The spirits have abandoned us."

That night *Kupuri,* the life force, slowly left the people's weakened bodies. As all lay in their huts awaiting death, a vision came into the dreams of Fast as Deer.

While Fast as Deer walked in the world of dreams, he saw that the sacred eagle flew in a circle above him. He felt the soft touch of a feather falling from the sky and landing upon his forehead. Then the sacred eagle spoke closely into his ear, "To end the drought, you must make four spears and cast each one into the four corners of earth."

In the morning Fast as Deer went and told the Mara'kame, "The sacred eagle has spoken to me in my dreams." But the Mara'kame, now old and weak, had forgotten about his own dream of long ago when he had searched for the boy's name.

"Ah! Young man, but you do not speak the language of the spirits. How could you understand the sacred eagle's voice?" he asked in disbelief.

"Its voice told me to hurl four spears, one to each corner of the earth to end the drought," Fast as Deer insisted.

"Your mind has become too weak without food and water. You must ignore your dreams," responded the Mara'kame.

Fast as Deer returned to his hut and tried to forget his vision as the holy man had ordered. But each night the sacred eagle kept returning to his dreams. "To end the drought, you must make four spears and cast each into the four corners of the earth," its voice repeated.

When dawn came on the fifth day, Fast as Deer finally decided to follow the sacred eagle's command. While his parents and the others lay too weak to rise, he walked away and carved four spears from the branches of a tree. He also attached eagle feathers to the end of each spear in honor of the sacred eagle.

As the new day began, Fast as Deer faced toward the sacred land of Wiricuta. With all his might he threw the first spear to the south. The spear cut through the wind, and as it fell to earth a fresh and cooling breeze began to blow over the desert floor.

Fast as Deer hurled the second spear to the north. After it landed on the ground the people were soon awakened by lightning and rumbling thunder. As they peeked through their doors, all saw how he cast the third spear toward the east. They followed the spear with their eyes. When it fell back to the earth, all saw that it brought the awaited, life-giving rain. The people rejoiced greatly as raindrops began pouring from the sky, bringing an end to the long drought.

"Ah! Fast as Deer has saved us from death," they exclaimed.

"Let us all go and thank him properly," said the Mara'kame.

But when the people came to him, they noticed that Fast as Deer held yet a fourth spear in his hand. "We thank you for saving us and our children from our deaths," the Mara'kame said. "I see that you hold one more spear in your hands," he added.

"You must cast it to the wind as you did with the others!" the people demanded. They wanted to know what the last spear would bring to the earth.

While everyone waited anxiously, Fast as Deer cast the fourth spear toward the west. They followed with their eyes as it traveled across the sky and disappeared from their sight. It seemed like a long time until they heard it falling back to the ground. Then all saw what the last spear had brought. The people held their breath and stared at the beautiful arch of seven colors that appeared in the sky, spreading across the land from one end to the other. "Ah!" the people exclaimed, as no one had ever seen anything so beautiful on earth.

"Let us go and chase after it!" a young man shouted.

"It could be a trap of evil doing," an elder warned.

A great fear took over the men, women, and children. Who would now go and find out what the strange and magical sight in the sky really was? But no one seemed to have the courage to go near it.

"Fast as Deer is the one who brought the arch of colors with his fourth spear," the Mara'kame reminded the others. "He must go and find out if the arch of colors is of danger to us."

Fast as Deer stood without moving. He heard how everyone agreed with the holy man. But for the first time he was overcome with great fear. His heart pounded as he heard the people shouting, "Go, Fast as Deer! You must go and find out what your last spear brought to the earth!"

Finally, while everyone watched, Fast as Deer slowly stepped away toward the mysterious arch of seven colors. After the people had long lost sight of him, he finally arrived at its foot. As he came closer, he saw that each color formed a step up into the sky. Suddenly Fast as Deer was no longer afraid, and up and up he began to climb. With every step he took, he saw the earth spreading below. And as he kept ascending, his arms slowly began to take the shape of the sacred eagle's wings. His feet also curled into sharp claws. But all along, Fast as Deer kept climbing up the steps, higher and higher into the sky.

When he finally reached the top, the magical ladder at once disappeared into the air. Fast as Deer then saw that he could roam with the flight of the sacred eagle, over the clouds and across the sky. He flew in circles above the awaiting people and heard the wind bringing their cheering voices to his ears. "Fast as Deer is the one who saved us from dying! He is the chosen one, the one who shares the spirit of the sacred eagle!" the people shouted to one another as he soared into the heavenly heights.

This legend speaks of Fast as Deer, as he lived in the memories of the forefathers. It tells of how this courageous young man rescued them from the long drought. And of how he was chosen by the sacred eagle and taken to live among the spirits in the heavens.

After each rain the magical arch still speaks of Fast as Deer as it spreads its glowing colors across the sky of Wiricuta, the sacred land of the Huichols.

The Huichols

The Huichols inhabit the rough terrain near the Sierra Madre Mountains in western México. At present the number of the tribe is estimated at 18,000. Their native tongue derives from *Nahuatl,* the Aztec language.

Their culture and customs are greatly influenced by ancient religious and spiritual beliefs. According to their forefathers, the gods created the Huichols in Wiricuta, the sacred land that lays at the center of earth. They also believe they are the only survivors of the Great Flood and are devoted worshipers of *Takauyasi,* Father Sun, and *Tatewari,* Grandfather Fire.

Following an ancient ritual that they believe ensures the survival of the world and all peoples, the Huichols travel once a year to the sacred land of Wiricuta to pay tribute to the gods. Guided by the *Mara'kame,* or holy man, the pilgrims carry their offerings, walking single file into Wiricuta, hundreds of miles away from their home. Many men, women, and children join the long journey. The yearly pilgrimage and their offerings prevent the sun from dying and the world from coming to an end.

The Huichols are highly creative and skilled in the arts of weaving and embroidery, and they are widely known for their colorful and exquisite yarn paintings.

Tahui

A Tarahumara Legend

"The time has come for the birth of your child." Nahaci awoke as she heard Mother Mountain whispering the words into her ears. Nahaci silently walked away from the rock shelter into the darkness of the forest. She reached the tree that she had chosen earlier and began to make a bed of dry grass and leaves. When she finished, she stood still in the center of it. Nahaci patiently awaited the sign from the round and glowing moon above. She was glad, for the coming of her child under a full moon was a good omen.

The child was born at dawn. Nahaci embraced him in her arms. Brushing away the dry leaves from his body, she spoke the legend of how the Tarahumara came to be. "We, the Tarahumara people, were sent to the earth from the sky," she whispered. She told him how in the beginning, the gods also sent from the heavens the gift of maize as their food. Her child must always be grateful for the kindness of the gods.

When the sun rose above the mountain, Nahaci returned to the shelter with the newborn in her arms. As she gave him to his father, Hunem, he saw with pride that his firstborn was a male child. "One day, my son, you will become a great Tarahumara runner," Hunem said as he held the child in his arms.

Three days later, Hunem took his son to the edge of the plateau. In the ancient custom of his ancestors, he offered the newborn to the Father of Light. "Mighty Father," he spoke in gratitude as he raised the child above his shoulders, "accept my son as your own child."

Later, when the sun disappeared below the horizon, Hunem walked toward the mountain where the spirits of higher thinking would give a name to his child. After five days and nights had passed, the spirits finally spoke. When Hunem returned he told the others, "Tahui, the word that means 'great child,' will be the name of my son."

When Tahui was five harvests old and his legs had grown strong enough, Nahaci spoke with Hunem. "The time has come for our son to join you in the hunt," she said. Once again Hunem was filled with pride. He would now teach his son the old ways, those which had been passed on to him from the forefathers.

The next day after Tahui had dressed in a white loincloth and headband, his mother spoke to him. "You will now help your father with the hunting."

As the sun began to hide behind the canyon walls, Tahui followed proudly at his father's side. They walked deep into the reed fields in search of small prey. Hunem and Nahaci knew their child's legs would become stronger from the hunting walks. For one day, once he became fifteen harvests of age, he must compete in the race to become a Rarámuri, one of the chosen men who became the mightiest foot runners of all the Tarahumara.

Every evening Tahui and his father went hunting in the canyon. When Tahui became tired his father would say, "I will tell you the story of Mother Mountain." At other times during the hunting journeys, Hunem told Tahui tales about the sky, the moon, and the stars. Hunem's intent was to make him forget about his tiredness. In this way his legs would become accustomed to the long walks. "One day, my child, you will run with the strength of the great foot runners," Hunem reassured him as they hunted under the stars. Tahui began dreaming of one day becoming a Rarámuri.

One evening when Tahui was seven harvests of age, the men returned in silence from the fishing journey. Tahui saw that his father was not among them. Soon the Shaman came and told Nahaci somberly, "The spirits of the river have called for Hunem." Nahaci remained silent, realizing Hunem was now gone forever. Tahui stared at her with saddened, teary eyes. He was too young to understand the passing of people into the next life, but he knew that without his father, life would never again be the same.

The next day when the light of dawn appeared in the sky, Hunem's body was buried inside a rock shelter. His clothing, hunting weapons, water, and food were all placed next to him. "His grave must be provided with plenty," the Shaman ordered. The Spirit of Hunem would need his belongings for the long journey into the Land of the Dead, where the shadows of night became their day and the moon took the place of the sun.

After the burial the Shaman returned to Nahaci and her child. "You must find a new shelter, for this place now belongs to the spirits," he said. So the people helped Nahaci and her son find a new cave where they would remain until the sign for the planting season came.

When the earth grew warmer and the flocks of birds returned, the tribe moved up onto the plateaus of the higher canyon. There they found the soil that was good for the maize crops. The people worked hard during the planting season, planting maize, squash, and beans. If the spirits of the rain were kind to their crops, the harvest would provide them with plenty. If they were not, hunger would follow and many would perish.

During the planting season, Tahui rose at dawn to help his mother in the fields. As night fell, the boys his age followed their fathers in the hunting. Tahui felt lonely. He sat by the river while the coyotes sang to the night shadows. As Tahui glanced at the moon and the stars above the sky, he thought of the stories Hunem had told him. The memories always made him feel close to his father. But as Tahui grew older, the memories grew distant until one day they finally faded. His legs had also become thin and weak, unlike those of the other boys, whose legs continued to strengthen during the hunting journeys.

When Tahui turned eleven harvests old, his weak legs became prey to the evil spirits of illness. One morning he awoke with a burning fever and great pains that did not allow him to rise from his bed. His mother sent for the Medicine Man. "Make my child walk again," she pleaded.

For many days the Medicine Man struggled against the spirits of the illness. He fought with the knowledge of medicinal herbs that had been passed on to him by the ancient healers. But he did not succeed. "The spirits of his illness are too strong to counter," the Medicine Man told Nahaci. "Your son may never be whole again."

Tahui lay in the darkness of the cave for many days and nights. The pain in his legs was so great that he had to walk with the shuffling steps of an old man. Tahui worried, as he now could not help his mother in the fields. But most of all he worried that he would not be able to participate in the Great Race when he turned fifteen harvests old. It was the duty of every male to compete at that age, and those who succeeded by finishing the race would be rewarded with manhood. Tahui's fear increased with each new harvest season as the drums called upon all who had turned fifteen harvests old.

One day Tahui heard the drums echoing across the canyon walls. "All those who will soon be fifteen harvests old must prepare for the Great Race," the drums announced. This time Tahui understood the message was for him. He knew he must begin preparing with the others so that he could also achieve the honor of becoming a man.

That morning Tahui spoke with his mother. "I must join the others and prepare for the Great Race," he said. Nahaci became sad as she remembered the words of the Medicine Man.

"My son," Nahaci responded, "the gods have traced a difficult task for you." She feared his illness would not allow him to succeed in the arduous run.

"I will prepare with the others," Tahui replied. He knew he must join them in the pursuit of manhood or be doomed to live in shame among his own people.

"May the gods bless you and strengthen your desire," his mother said in consent.

The following day, as the rising sun painted the sky with crimson streaks, Tahui joined the others. The boys laughed when they saw his thin and deformed legs. "Your weak legs will not carry you far," many teased.

"His illness will not allow him to earn his manhood," others whispered. Tahui felt great sadness and shame as he overheard their words. He quietly returned to his shelter, but he was not discouraged.

"I must prepare alone. The others will not laugh at my crippled legs again," he informed his mother.

While the people slept in their shelters, Tahui quietly crept toward the dusty and lonely trail. Surrounded by the night shadows, he began the slow and painful run. Every night while the others slept, Tahui trained. As he ran on the trail he forced himself to ignore the pain in his legs. "Running will make my legs strong and fast," he repeated to himself each time he began his lonely practice. He stayed away from the others until the awaited harvest arrived, when the boys his age would compete in the Great Race.

The day before the race the Shaman went into every shelter. One by one he spoke to each runner. "The gods will reward you with the gift of manhood after you finish the Great Race," he encouraged them. When the Shaman arrived at Nahaci's cave, he was overcome with sorrow by Tahui's crippled legs. He did not repeat the words of encouragement he had given the others. "May the spirit of the great Rarámuri guide you and give you strength," he only said, for he believed this weak and crippled boy would not succeed in the long race.

That night, as was the custom before the race, Nahaci rubbed her son's legs with herb oils and teas. When dawn approached, the beat of the drums again resounded across the canyon. This time they called the names of each runner, but Tahui's name was not called along with the others. He wore a white loincloth and headband. His mother gave him a pair of rawhide sandals that had belonged to his father. Tahui then walked toward the meeting place at the foot of the hills.

When Tahui arrived, he saw that the fathers and brothers of the other runners had also come along. They would wait at the foothills for those who would be blessed by finishing the Great Race. The other boys hurriedly attached the belts with deer hooves onto their waists and ankles as their fathers and brothers had once worn themselves. The deer hooves would give the young runners the strength and speed of the deer, and would also keep them awake at night during the long and strenuous race. Tahui wore none. He stood alone awaiting the start.

As the sun appeared over the mountain peak, the Shaman announced the start of the race. Every boy who was fifteen harvests of age began the long run in his pursuit of manhood.

One runner, then another, and many others soon passed Tahui. When the sun reached mid-sky and burned with the fury of a roaring beast, the other runners had left Tahui far behind. Although his legs ached and beads of sweat dripped from his face, his desire for the honor of manhood gave him the strength to keep running. As the sun sank into the canyon his pain and weakness increased. Dust and sweat covered his entire body.

When darkness came, Tahui lumbered in slow and painful steps. He now knew he would not finish the Great Race just as the others had teased. In defeat, Tahui stopped running. He sadly dragged his feet along the road. "I must search for a memory that will keep away the pain and weakness," he gasped in a last effort. To encourage himself, he thought of the kindness of the gods, the beauty of the canyon, and many other memories. But none helped him. Thinking of the dishonor and shame of not attaining manhood, Tahui raised his teary eyes. He silently stared at the moon and the stars above.

Suddenly, the words came to him, "One day, my child, you will become a great runner." Tahui heard the words that his father had told him during their hunting journeys. And for the first time in many harvests, the long-lost memories returned. Tahui felt the presence of his father's spirit as his words grew louder above the heavens: "You will become a great runner." The pain and weakness slowly disappeared. And soon he began to run with the speed of the deer and the swiftness of the eagle as the spirit of Hunem ran by his side.

As dawn approached Tahui reached and passed the nearest runner, then another, and many others. Soon all the runners were left behind as Tahui led the race.

When the sun again appeared over the mountain peak, the waiting crowd spotted a lone runner far in the distance. "He is coming! The first runner is coming!" all shouted in excitement. A chatter also spread as the lone runner came closer to the foothills.

"Is he my son?" each father asked with hope.

"It must be my brother!" the boys anxiously told one another. A gasp soon rose among the crowd.

"It is Tahui! It is the one who could not run!"

Tahui was the first to reach the foothills where all the others waited. As he arrived everyone saw that his legs were now strong and healthy, like those of the great Rarámuri. The gods had been touched by Tahui's great effort and struggle against

his own pain and weakness. Along with the gift of manhood, the gods had returned health and strength to his legs.

In time, Tahui became the greatest Rarámuri among the chosen runners of the Tarahumara tribe.

The Tarahumaras

The Tarahumaras inhabit an extensive and isolated region of the Occidental Mountain Range in the northern state of Chihuahua, México.

The Tarahumaras number approximately 60,000 and are considered one of the largest and most primitive tribes in the North American continent. They form part of the Uto-Aztec linguistic group and are related to the Apaches of the southwestern United States. The two main features for which they are known worldwide are the preservation of their ancient culture and their outstanding ability as endurance runners. They also are one of the few existing seminomadic cave dwellers.

The Tarahumaras' main source of food is corn, which they cook in various forms. They also cultivate beans, squash, and peppers and make extensive use of wild plants for food and medicinal purposes. Hunting of small game and deer is another important source of food. Their ancient method of deer hunting is by chasing the animal nonstop for several days until it collapses from exhaustion.

The Tarahumaras practice running from early childhood and are considered the greatest endurance runners in the world. They call their best runners *Rarámuri,* or foot runners, and have participated since 1926 in major world running events.

The Boy Who Cried Tears of Jade

A Mayan Legend

Mayel lived with her family in the outskirts of the great city of Tikal. Every morning while her father and brothers worked in the maize fields, she and her sister helped their mother tend the garden of squash and beans. At dusk the family ate their evening meal by the dim light of the fire. This was Mayel's favorite time, for she was able to listen to her parents' stories and later play games with her brothers and sister.

Mayel was aware that her childhood would soon end. After she turned twelve years old she would join her grandmother, the Medicine Woman. Following the custom of the forefathers, on the day of Mayel's birth the priests had planned her destiny according to the stars in the heavens. She was chosen to follow the steps of her grandmother, and in time she would become the next healer.

The day before she reached the awaited birthday, her mother called upon her. "My dear daughter," she began, "you were born under the sign of Ixchel, the moon and Goddess of Medicine. Tomorrow when the sun rises in the east you will start a new life."

The next morning while Mayel was gathering her belongings, she heard the hollow knocks. Before opening the door she already knew that the visitor was Itzá, her grandmother. The old woman wore a black robe and carried on her arm a woven basket filled with herbs. "My child, you are now entering womanhood," Itzá said. "As of today you shall come and live with me. This basket which I now carry will someday belong to you." Like Itzá and all the medicine women before her, Mayel's learning must now begin.

After her family bid her farewell, Mayel and her grandmother went along a narrow and winding trail up toward the slopes. "Those," Itzá said, pointing her finger at a patch of bushes covered with small white and yellow flowers, "Those are the good healers of stomach pains, but its blossoms must be collected before the end of the rains." Then, pinching a sample of the shrub, she rubbed it in her hands and brought it to Mayel's nose. In this way Mayel would also learn to identify the plant by its smell. The first lesson had begun.

When they arrived at Itzá's hut, Mayel's eyes widened with curiosity as she entered the small room. Roots and herbs hung in several rows from the ceiling and walls, and a sweet fragrance of wild fruits and dried flowers filled the air. At dusk, before the evening meal, Mayel and her grandmother knelt at the center of the room. While Itzá burned incense to the nine lords of the night, she began the story about the first healer woman. "After the gods made the flesh of our ancestors from maize, men, women, and children fell prey to disease and pain. No one had the knowledge to cure their ills, and for a long time many died. One day Ixchel took pity on the people. She came down from the sky and took a woman with her back to the heavens. There she taught her all of her medicinal knowledge. When the chosen woman returned to earth, she began to cure the sick. With herbs and roots she made them well again. Before joining the ancestors, she passed her knowledge on to the next woman who was born under the sign of the merciful Ixchel. I received this same knowledge from the healer before me. It is now my duty to pass it on to you," Itzá concluded.

As Mayel lay in her wooden bed, she thought about how lucky she was. One day she would share the healing knowledge of the goddess Ixchel, and with it she would cure the ills of her people.

Every day Mayel and her grandmother browsed through the forest and fields. Each carried a basket in which they gathered healing herbs and roots. At dusk, after they shared a meal of boiled beans and corn cakes, Itzá taught Mayel the names and curing powers of the herbs and roots they had collected. She also told her stories about the ancestors and the great rulers of the past.

One evening after finishing the first cycle of learning, while Mayel lay asleep, the old Medicine Woman silently worked by the fire. She gathered a small pile of clay and mixed it with water until it turned into soft mud. Then she began molding the clay into the body of a male child. She carefully shaped its head, arms, and legs, and made its eyes with two green chips of jade. She then placed the doll into the fire. The flames danced in its shiny green eyes while the body hardened.

The next morning after Mayel awoke, she smiled when she discovered her grandmother's gift laying at her bedside. "Thank you, grandmother!" she exclaimed. Turning to the doll, Mayel said joyfully, "You will be my new friend."

Mayel took her doll everywhere she went. She held it under her arm or carried it in the basket of herbs while she followed her grandmother's steps. After returning to the hut, while Itzá rested, Mayel played outside with the doll until the evening star appeared in the west. "I wish you could speak and run just like I do," she often said to her doll.

One day when Mayel and her grandmother returned from the forest, dark clouds quickly covered the sky. Soon a pouring rain began to fall. As the two hurried into the hut, the doll fell from Mayel's basket. While they slept, the doll lay outside in the cold and rainy night.

Near dawn, before the evening star disappeared, the doll of clay slowly came to life. As the last raindrops fell upon the forest, the male child rose to his feet and rubbed his eyes, as if awakening from a long sleep.

After Mayel awoke she discovered that her doll was not in the basket. She quickly began to look for it. When she opened the door and stepped outside, instead of her doll she found a child with bright green eyes standing on the wet grass. "Grand-mother!" Mayel cried out.

Itzá peeked out the door and saw that the doll of clay was now a human boy. "You will be my brother," Mayel happily blurted.

"You will live with us. Your name shall be Balam." Itzá gave him the name that meant "sacred jaguar," for the child's eyes were as green as those of the jungle cat.

Balam now came along into the forest, helping Mayel and her grandmother collect the healing herbs. In the evenings while the old Medicine Woman rested, he and Mayel kept each other company. She taught him to whistle the song of the quetzal bird and all the games she once played with her brothers and sister.

One afternoon while the two ran in the fields, Balam stumbled on the root of a tree and crumbled to the ground. As he rose he felt a sharp pain in his leg and his knee began to bleed. Having never known pain, Balam burst into sobs. But his tears were not like those of Mayel or any other person on earth. As his teardrops slid down his face and fell to the ground, they turned into green beads of jade.

Startled, Mayel picked up the exquisite jewels, grabbed Balam by the hand and hurried back to the hut. "These are Balam's tears," she told her grandmother, showing her the beads.

With great wonder Itzá held the jewels close to her eyes. Balam's teardrops had indeed become fine pieces of jade. She smiled as she spoke to him. "You have been blessed with a special gift. We shall find a way to share it with others," Itzá said. For jade was a favorite offering that the people often sought for the mighty rulers and the gods. As the time of paying the yearly tribute approached, Itzá now knew what she should do with Balam's tears.

That evening while Itzá knelt by the fire and told Balam and Mayel stories about the ancestors, she strung the jade beads into a beautiful necklace. Once finished, she carefully wrapped it with corn husks. "This will be our offering," she said proudly.

When the awaited day arrived, Itzá journeyed with her offering into the city of Tikal. But this time, instead of bringing a basket of scented flowers and medicinal herbs and teas, the healer woman carried the jade necklace. She followed the crowds of merchants and farmers who also came, bringing presents of seeds, fine weavings, and feathers. Itzá waited in the long line of peasants. When her turn came, she handed her offering to the ruler traders. They then gave her a chip that bore the royal symbol as proof of having fulfilled her duty.

Later the ruler and his wife strolled about the enormous piles of tributes. Curious about the strange bundle of corn husks among all the other gifts, the two quickly unwrapped the jade necklace. "Never have I seen such exquisitely crafted jewels!" she exclaimed.

"I shall provide you with many more of these," the ruler responded. Then he wrapped the necklace back in the corn husks and called upon the traders.

"You must find the giver of this offering!" he demanded.

"It was the old Medicine Woman who brought that gift," said a man after he recognized the wrapping.

The ruler quickly sent his soldiers to search for the healer. Soon the men dressed in jaguar skins and fancy feathers and pendants showed up at Itzá's door. "Our Lord wishes for more of your jewels."

"I own no more of those," Itzá responded. Noticing greed in the men's eyes, she began to fear for Balam. Itzá realized she must not reveal the secret.

"Let us in! We must find out if your words are true," the men demanded. Storming inside the hut, they searched in every corner but soon became discouraged. They could not find even a trace of the precious jewels.

"You must come along with us. You will be imprisoned until you tell us your secret," the soldiers shouted. Trembling in a corner, Balam and Mayel saw how the wicked men forced Itzá away. The two helplessly burst into tears.

"Look!" a soldier shouted. "Come and look at the boy's tears!"

The men gathered around Balam. With great surprise all saw how his teardrops turned into the desired green beads of jade as they fell to the ground. "The child with green eyes is the maker of the jewels. We must bring him with us."

Two men carried the tearful and frightened Balam back to the palace. The others followed behind, picking up his tears that had turned into beads of jade. Meanwhile, Itzá watched helplessly as Mayel sobbed, "My brother is gone!" The old Medicine Woman feared that Balam was gone forever.

At dusk the soldiers arrived at the palace with Balam. They told the ruler about the magical tears and proudly showed him and his wife the handfuls of jewels they had collected along the way. "The child shall never leave my domain," the merciless ruler instructed the men.

Balam was thrown into a cold, dark cell. Every night he curled up, shivering in a corner. While he stared through the small window at the evening star, he thought of Itzá and Mayel. "I will never see Grandmother and Mayel again," he wept. But his crying only pleased the greedy ruler and his wife.

"The more tears he sheds, the more jewels we will own," they happily concluded.

As the days passed, the Medicine Woman and Mayel searched for a way to free Balam. Every evening after the sun died in the west, Itzá made her offering of incense to the nine lords of the night and asked for their help. "Mighty lords, help me find a way to rescue Balam," she prayed. Many days and nights passed until the nine lords finally answered her pleas and appeared in her dreams amidst a cloud of smoke.

"After the evening star appears in the sky," they said, "go into the forest and find a mangrove tree. Brew its roots into a potion and bring it to your child. He must drink it when the moon is whole, and then he will be set free."

Early the next evening, Itzá and Mayel hurried to the swamps where the mangrove trees grew. When they returned to the hut the Medicine Woman boiled the roots as told in her dream. For many days the two waited anxiously.

When the full moon finally appeared, Itzá and Mayel traveled among the shadows of the night. They carefully carried the potion in a sealed conch shell. After reaching the palace, Itzá quietly instructed Mayel. "There is not much time left. We must find Balam before dawn." Protected by the darkness, they sneaked from one corner to another, clinging their bodies to the stone walls. But as time passed and dawn slowly approached, the Medicine Woman began to lose hope of ever finding Balam.

Then Mayel paused as she remembered the song of the quetzal that she had taught Balam. She silently crept ahead of her grandmother. Bringing both hands close to her lips, she began to blow through her fingers. Mayel gently whistled the song of the quetzal. Itzá followed close behind while Mayel slipped from wall to wall, calling Balam with her whistling sound.

Balam lay asleep in a corner of his cell, but he quickly awoke when Mayel's whistle reached his ears. After he peeked through the window bars, he discovered Itzá and Mayel searching for him in the moonlight. Balam hurriedly responded by whistling back the song of the quetzal. When the Medicine Woman and Mayel looked up at the tower, they saw Balam as he waved his arms with joy.

"We must find a way to get the potion to him," the old woman said. Mayel crept over to a tree that grew near Balam's tower. Carefully holding the sealed container in her hand, she swiftly clambered up the branches. Once she reached the small window, she slipped the conch shell through the wooden bars. "Hurry! Drink this potion that grandmother has made for you. It will set you free," Mayel whispered.

Balam grasped the container in his hand, and while Mayel descended from the tree he drank its liquid at once.

Itzá and Mayel happily walked back to the hut while the last beams of the evening star glared in the dawning sky. Suddenly, a powerful roar rumbled throughout the forest. As it reached their ears, Itzá and Mayel realized that the magic potion had indeed worked.

Awakened by the loud roaring, the guards hurried to look into Balam's cell. They slowly opened the door, peeked inside and shuddered with fright. The boy was not in the cell. But in his place stood an enormous jaguar with eyes as green as the forest grass and fur as dark as the night. The fierce cat advanced threateningly, growling and baring its sharp teeth and claws. The guards dropped their weapons and shields, saying, "Quickly! Let's save ourselves from this evil beast!"

While the guards scrambled away, the jaguar escaped out of the cell and dashed through the palace halls. It sprang over fences and, after reaching the courtyard, climbed up a tree near the last wall. With a powerful leap, the jaguar broke away from the palace and into the safety of the forest, his new domain.

And every evening after, Itzá and Mayel heard Balam's voice as the powerful roar of the jaguar, the forest lord of the night.

The Mayas

The mighty Mayas, worshippers of the heavens and time, flourished between AD 300 and 900. As the most advanced astronomers, architects, mathematicians, and engineers of their time, they built a great empire in the heart of the jungle with splendid cities of stone. They also invented the most advanced and complicated writing system in the New World and a calendar nearly as accurate as our own.

The Mayas spread through southern México, Guatemala, Belize, and El Salvador. With a population of approximately

7 million, they remain one of the most numerous North American indigenous peoples. There are thirty Mayan dialects currently spoken among the various Mayan groups.

According to the ancient beliefs, the flesh of their ancestors was made from the sacred maize, and the stars in the heavens ruled their lives.

The time of the mighty rulers and kings for whom were built majestic pyramids and palaces is forever gone, but the Mayas today still follow many of the ways and rituals of their ancestors.

Tribe of the Deer

A Tarascan Legend

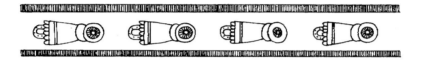

In the beginning, when the gods had forgotten about the earth, the first people lived in great hardship. Each day, the men and women roamed from one place to another in search of food and shelter. At night they shivered in the cold wind. In time many became ill and weak.

Thicatame, their leader, went and spoke to the High Priest. "Our suffering is too great," Thicatame complained.

"I will pray to the gods to show their mercy on us," the High Priest responded as he walked away toward the mountain. Without tasting food or water, day after day, he called upon the gods for help. "We have been forgotten here on earth," the High Priest pleaded. The wind brought the cry of the people up to Curicaveri's ears.

On the seventh day Curicaveri, the God of Fire, descended from the heavens and responded. "I shall end your suffering," he said. Out of his great kindness and love, the god gave the people the gift of fire.

"Tell the people to keep only one fire alive. Tell them to care for the trees that feed the fire," Curicaveri commanded.

"What will we have for food?" the High Priest asked. Curicaveri touched a cloud with his hands and seeds of corn and beans fell like rain.

"Plant these seeds over the fields. Tell the men and women to care for the plants that will sprout from them," he said before returning to the heavens.

In this way the first people ended their wandering and settled in a green valley. The seeds provided them with food as they cultivated the earth. They kept warm at night by creating a great fire near the shelter where they slept. For a long time the people lived in harmony and were grateful for the kind ways of the God of Fire.

"We must remind our children to live in the ways of Curicaveri," they vowed to one another.

But, as their children grew and went to work in the fields of corn and beans, one day the people of the second age began to complain among themselves. Soon they took their troubles to Zirám, the new leader.

"Our work is too hard. We are lonely in the fields," the people complained. Early the next morning, Zirám told the High Priest about the hardships of the young men and women.

"Call for the help of Curicaveri," Zirám commanded.

The holy man climbed to the top of the mountain. For days and nights he called with his prayers for the help of the God of Fire. On the seventh day, Curicaveri heard his calling and again returned to the earth.

"The work of the people is too hard. It makes them tired and lonely in the fields," complained the High Priest.

"I shall send help and companionship for them," responded Curicaveri.

In his great love and kindness, he once more helped the men and women. This time he brought to the earth the deer from the heavens. "Brother Deer shall help the people," Curicaveri instructed the High Priest.

Brother Deer became companion to the people in the long hours of harvest and helped by eating the grasses that grew in the corn and bean fields. The men and women again were grateful for the kindness of the God of Fire. And the people of the second age lived on the earth in harmony and peace beside Brother Deer.

But when their children grew and went to work in the fields, they also became discontented. "Why must we only feed from seeds?" many asked.

"Why must we live by only one fire?" others complained.

Tikámen, the third leader, soon went to the High Priest. "We need more food and more fires. Let us better our ways," he said. The High Priest agreed with him.

"We will no longer live by the old laws," Tikámen added. The men and women of the third age had forgotten their gratitude to Curicaveri.

The people soon dispersed into many shelters and everyone built a fire of his own. Their need for wood to feed all the fires now became greater. Many more trees were cut down by the ungrateful ones. The greedy hunters of the third age also began to kill Brother Deer with their weapons. They ate its flesh and wore its hide as clothing. All began to live by the new ways, with an abundance of food and fires their ancestors had not known.

The men and women multiplied on the earth and taught their children the new ways. Everyone had now forgotten about the commands of the God of Fire, all but Atzimba, the orphan girl who could not speak. Atzimba loved Brother Deer and spent the days alone in the green and quiet of the fields, where she hid from the others. There she played her flute all day. The song from her flute was the only sound she was able to make. Atzimba enjoyed sharing her music with Brother Deer, as they were the only ones who were not afraid to be near her. No one ever came close or spoke to her. "Her voice has been possessed by the evil spirits who live within her," they said.

"We must keep away from the one who has no voice," the men and women warned their children.

Atzimba was very lonely and suffered from the silence of the others. But she hurt even more seeing the hunters returning from the fields. They carried Brother Deer on their backs after killing it with their weapons. In silence she cried for the fate of her only friends.

One day, Atzimba saw that there were only a few deer left on the earth. "I must help the last of Brother Deer," Atzimba thought to herself. Grabbing her flute, she walked to the fields where Brother Deer grazed. She began to play her flute as she led the herd toward the top of the mountain. The deer leapt behind Atzimba, following her beautiful music that seemed to say, "Come with me and be safe." Fearing the evil of the others, Atzimba and the last of the deer crept away to live at the top of the mountain, far from the selfish people.

That evening no one noticed that the girl without a voice had disappeared. But the next day the greedy hunters returned empty-handed. "The deer have disappeared from the fields," they informed.

Later the fire-keepers also returned without bundles of wood. "There are no more trees. How will we feed our fires?" they complained.

After the deer were gone, countless weeds began to grow in the fields. Soon they overcame and buried the corn and bean plants. As the bad grasses spread, clouds of insects appeared. During many days and nights the swarms of hungry grasshoppers and locusts fed upon the fields of seed. The crops were soon destroyed. And the people once again began to suffer like the men and women of the first age. Without food they felt the pain of hunger. Without fire they shivered in the cold wind at night.

"You must ask Curicaveri to show mercy upon us," the men and women begged the High Priest.

At dawn he climbed the mountain and with his prayers began imploring the God of Fire for help. On the seventh day, Curicaveri again returned to earth.

"We are hungry and cold," the High Priest protested.

"Did not I send to earth the seed of corn and beans?" Curicaveri asked.

"Plagues of insects came upon the fields and ate our plants and seeds," he responded.

"Did not I give the first people fire for all to keep warm?" the God of Fire asked.

"We ran out of trees from which we fed our many fires," the High Priest explained. Curicaveri grew angry as he saw that the High Priest now wore the horns of Brother Deer upon his head and its hide over his body. "Did I not order you to live with the deer as brothers?" he demanded.

"We are much too great to live by your unjust ways," the High Priest shouted in defiance as he turned his back on Curicaveri and returned to the people. "Curicaveri is a merciless god. He is unfair to his people," he said to them.

When evening came and the children slept, the angered men and women conspired against Curicaveri. "The God of Fire is not worthy of our love. We must bring death to him," the maddened crowd decided.

The fighters gathered their bows and arrows. The women painted the weapons in red, black, and yellow, which were the sacred colors of the gods. When the warriors were ready for battle, they followed the High Priest toward the mountain. They hid behind the bushes while the High Priest called upon the God of Fire.

When Curicaveri descended from the heavens, the angry men sprang from their hiding places. For many days they waged war against Curicaveri, darkening the sun with their arrows. The God of Fire stood erect. From dawn to dusk his body slowly became covered with the arrows painted with the sacred colors. On the ninth day, when all the warriors became tired and began running out of weapons, Curicaveri finally fell to the earth. The sky on the horizon became reddened with his blood. And the mountains and plains shook as the weight of his body crashed to the ground.

At dusk the warriors returned from the mountain. "Our merciless god has fallen," they told the waiting women. The men and women went to rest in their shelters, rejoicing in their victory over Curicaveri. But the earth still kept rumbling from the agonizing cry of the fallen god.

At dawn the children were awakened by Curicaveri's last breath. When they saw his blood splashed across the sky, they became ashamed and saddened at their parents' greed. "Our parents have angered the gods," the children said while the plains shook with greater force. "We must ask their forgiveness."

The men and women stayed hidden in their shelters, too frightened to come out and face the fury of the gods. Meanwhile, the children walked across the plains. Together they cut flowers of all the colors that grew on the prairie. One after another they marched in a long line, carrying their offerings toward the dying god. The children grew even sadder as they came near Curicaveri and saw the evil their fathers and mothers had done.

"Forgive our parents," the children begged. They washed away the blood of Curicaveri with their tears and buried his body with the beautiful flowers from the prairie.

Meanwhile, the insides of the earth kept roaring and trembling over the hills and valleys. And the ground where Curicaveri lay grew into a tall mountain of smoke and fire.

From the top Atzimba saw how the anger of the mountain of smoke and fire was about to fall upon the people. "I must return and warn the others," she realized. But when Atzimba came down she had no words with which to warn the people about the danger they faced. And she saw that all of them still feared her.

Atzimba reached for her flute and began playing the song, for the music that came from her flute was the only sound she ever made. "Follow me to the safety of the mountain," her song seemed to say to the people.

The people became startled at the beautiful sound that traveled in the wind. They also understood that Atzimba was calling them along. Everyone followed her and the beautiful sound up to the top. Soon after, the angry and roaring mountain spat rivers of fire, burying the plains and the valleys. The people now understood that the girl without a voice had risked her own life to rescue them from death.

When the anger of the mountain of smoke and fire ended, the people turned toward Atzimba. They now realized that she had always lived in punishment and loneliness by their unjust and fearful ways.

"Will you forgive us?" the men and women pleaded.

"Will you return to live with us?" the children asked her. Atzimba agreed by softly nodding her head as a tear of joy slid down her face.

As Atzimba returned with the people to search for a new place, Brother Deer stayed behind on the top of the mount. The deer would now live under the watchful eyes and protection of the gods.

Now a smile shone on Atzimba's face. She felt truly happy realizing that she would no longer live in loneliness and silence. For the first time, Atzimba knew she belonged with the others.

The Tarascos

The Tarascos inhabit the northern mountains and lakeshores in the state of *Michoacán,* or Land of Fishermen. Although the origin of this tribe has not been clearly established, Lake Pátzcuaro is known as the capital of the Tarasco empire. While most tribes of Mesoamerica paid tribute to the Aztecs, the legendary Tarasco warriors were among the few tribes who were not conquered by the powerful Aztec armies.

The Tarascos live primarily by agriculture, fishing, and small-game hunting. They demonstrate a unique artistry in working with gold, silver, and copper. They are also experts in the arts of pottery and woodcarving with an exquisite lacquer finish.

The shy but dignified Tarascos still live in close contact with nature along the shores of Lake Pátzcuaro and in adjacent villages.

Legend of the Feathered Serpent

An Aztec Legend

The old warrior who had fought many battles sat by his earthen fire. The children knelt around him as he began the legend.

"The year One Reed is near," he said, "and Quetzalcóatl, the Feathered Serpent, God of Life and Learning, will fulfill his promise by returning to this, his land. He will soon come back from the sea in a floating raft and reclaim his power and his people." The children listened to his words without making a sound or movement. The mighty Feathered Serpent, the god whom their parents and the people before them spoke of for so long, was finally coming. The end was near. And in the last days all lived in fear.

But no one in the Aztec empire knew of greater fear than Moctezuma, the mighty emperor. Moctezuma lived in a palace as large as a city. He was surrounded by forests and beautiful gardens in which quetzals, parrots, and other colorful birds flew about the bushes and trees. The grounds were covered with many kinds of flowers whose sweet scent spread with the wind.

Moctezuma rested every afternoon in his favorite courtyard where pumas, jaguars, and tigers roamed inside large wooden cages. At mealtimes the servants paraded around his table with hundreds of different dishes. But now, in the last days, all of his pleasures were forgotten. The song of his beloved birds, the exquisite perfume from his gardens, and the flavorful feasts no longer provided Moctezuma with joy or pleasure. The voices of the prophecy haunted his long days and sleepless nights.

One day a ball of fire appeared across the sky and burned throughout the night. The noblemen, wizards, and priests came to Moctezuma with concern. "Great Lord," a priest warned, "strange signs and omens are appearing on earth and in the sky."

"The people are awakened at night by strange howls and cries," a nobleman reported.

"Our nights are plagued with horrible dreams and visions," a wizard complained. The mighty ruler listened while he sadly stared through the window at his beloved city of Tenochtitlan. When the men finished speaking, Moctezuma remained silent for a long time.

"Do not be afraid," he finally said to them. "You must re-member that all which begins also comes to an end. I, the ruler of this great empire, shall guide my people in the last days." Moctezuma knew his days of glory and power would soon be over, but his people must not witness his trembling.

Moctezuma stayed alone in his sleeping chamber. With sharp needles from the agave cactus, he pierced his body in sacrifice to the gods. He did not eat or drink, so that he could purify himself by fasting.

Many days later he sent for all of his helpers. When the servants and wizards, the priests and noblemen came to his calling, they saw that he looked very thin, and that he had not bathed for many days. "We shall prepare to welcome the Feathered Serpent, who will soon take my place," Moctezuma instructed.

At dawn the people were awakened by a call from conch shells that resounded across and beyond Tenochtitlan. Everyone rose and hurried to the palace. "Why is it that we are awakened at this early hour?" they wondered along the way.

When the large crowds arrived at the palace doors, Moctezuma himself came out and said, "He who left to the east is coming back. And after the great Feathered Serpent returns, I, Moctezuma, shall no longer rule."

"Will he be angry at us and our children? Will he take revenge upon us?" the crowd asked. For according to the legend, the Feathered Serpent had left greatly displeased with the forefathers. One day he grew angry at their ways of human sacrifices and wars. With great discontent he went away on a raft of snakes and disappeared into the eastern waters.

Moctezuma again spoke to the crowds as he noticed fear in their words. "The Feathered Serpent must be loved and respected. We shall obey his ways and avoid all that may displease him or provoke his wrath," he warned.

As the year One Reed began, Moctezuma grew more anxious with each day that passed. One morning while he looked at the new blossoms in the gardens, a servant came to him. "One of your guardians of the water's shores has come to speak with you," he said. But before the man who had come from the coast spoke, Moctezuma already knew what his message would be.

"Oh, Great Lord," he said, "we have seen over the waters of the east floating rafts as big as many houses." As soon as the messenger left, Moctezuma called his noblemen.

"You must find an offering worthy of the mighty Feathered Serpent," he ordered. Soon the best workers of jewels, metals, clothing, and feathers were brought to him. For many days and nights, the jewelers created exquisite gifts of gems, turquoise, and jade. The goldsmiths carved bracelets and pendants adorned with mother-of-pearl. The weavers spun the finest clothes, and a crown of quetzal feathers was made for the returning one. Once the offerings were finished, Moctezuma led his helpers and noblemen to welcome the long-awaited god.

After a tiring journey, the Aztec emperor finally came face to face with the bearded god and his followers. The bearded god, guarded closely by his men, approached Moctezuma. Many of his men were mounted on four-legged beasts never before seen in the land. The bearded god and his companions were dressed in strange clothing with metal parts. They held their weapons as if they were ready to strike.

When Moctezuma and the bearded god stood within arm's length, the emperor's servants laid the offerings at the feet of the god. And they saw with relief that the gifts pleased him greatly, for his face lit up with a smile. Then Moctezuma, the owner of glory and power that had known no limits, spoke with a low and humble voice. "Oh, Mighty One, the long-awaited Feathered Serpent, I am your servant, the honored one who was chosen to guard your kingdom and your people. We cherish your return. May our gifts be to your pleasing. May you and your followers rest your tired feet from the long travel to this, your land."

The bearded one and his men did not understand the strange language of the leader who wore a large headdress of feathers and fancy clothing. But they spoke in their own words amongst themselves. And all along, their eyes preyed upon the gifts of precious metals and jewels as the thirsty traveler craves water to quench his thirst.

Moctezuma and his men escorted the bearded one and his people back to the palace. Along the way the Aztec emperor instructed his helpers, "Behold the mighty one, and be assured that he and his companions are fed and clothed properly." And as they arrived, in the last days of peace, the wind grew still in the great Tenochtitlan. Many of the old women and men did not rejoice at the coming of the strangers. But they wept and prayed to the gods for the fate of their sons and daughters.

"What evil fate has fallen upon us?" the elders worried.

As the days passed the people became more trusting of the ones who had come in the floating rafts. They saw that the men greeted them with broad smiles and held their hands and patted their backs in a strange manner. But the more gifts and offerings the men received, the faster they changed their ways. They soon began to make more demands, and when not pleased, they lashed their whips upon the men and women.

Many of the people brought their complaints to Moctezuma. "Must you allow the unkindness of the bearded men toward us?" they asked.

"We should not anger the Feathered Serpent and his soldiers. But we shall please them and obey their ways," Moctezuma responded.

"Are you no longer our lord, the one who rules over us?"

"The mighty Quetzalcóatl now sits at my throne. He is the new lord and ruler of us all," he reminded them. The people turned their backs after he spoke. They returned to the city in great disappointment.

The bearded one now realized that Moctezuma regarded him as the long-awaited god, and that he was greatly feared. He began instructing his men with his evil ways. Mounted on the four-legged beasts, he led them into the city carrying heavy maces and torches.

For many days and nights the evil men went into the temples and smashed their maces against the gods of stone. They broke into the houses of nobles and peasants and stuffed their saddle-bags with gold and jewels. With their torches they burned every book that told the story of the Aztec people and the ones who came before them. They tortured and imprisoned the men and women who stood in their way. The great Tenochtitlan soon was ablaze. And of all that its people held sacred or holy, nothing was left standing or whole.

As the bearded one and his men created a path of destruc-tion, the people understood that he was not a true god. He who was called the mighty Feathered Serpent by their ruler was but a mad and ruthless mortal.

A priest soon brought sad news to the people. "Our lord Moctezuma has perished because of the invaders. Those men are no longer worthy of our trust," he warned. His words soon spread to the farmers in a village near the city.

"We are at the mercy of the evil ones," cried a woman.

"We shall defend ourselves from the invaders!" a man shouted.

"But we cannot fight their fire-spitting weapons," said another.

"Xochipilli is in great danger," the singers, poets, and dancers realized. Word had come to them of how the bearded men were destroying all their gods and shrines. Everyone began to fear for Xochipilli, the God of Flowers and the Arts.

"Let us save our god," shouted Itauqui, or the devoted one. Itauqui, the young keeper of the temple of Xochipilli, vowed, "I shall guard his house day and night."

But it was not long before the evil men arrived in the village. One evening, Itauqui discovered the silhouette of the invaders creeping into the temple. He saw how the men sneaked silently, like thieves in the night.

Once the men were inside, they lit their torches and began searching. Soon they discovered the god of stone that was covered with flowers from its head to its feet. The men quickly raised their maces to crash them against the god.

Itauqui's body trembled with anger and he readied himself to strike against the perpetrators. Suddenly one of the men howled a strange cry. The others stopped and, lowering their maces, looked closer, circling tightly around Xochipilli. The men smiled wickedly as they saw what lay beneath the adorning flowers—the god's head was crowned with mother-of-pearl, a large heart made of gold was encrusted in his chest, and his body was clothed with gems and turquoise. The bearded thieves pointed with their fingers at the precious jewels. They muttered strange words that Itauqui could not understand. But he saw that the stare in their eyes was that of the hungry snake looking upon its prey.

The men desperately tried to remove the treasures from the god's body, but none of them succeeded. They whispered to one another and once again surrounded Xochipilli. Joining their strength, the evil ones tried to lift and drag the God of Flowers and the Arts away from his altar. But soon the men realized that the great statue of stone was much too heavy for them to carry. They went outside and quickly returned, bringing in their beasts along with thick ropes across their shoulders. They wrapped and knotted the ropes around the god and hitched the beasts to the statue and began tugging and pushing.

Hidden in one corner, Itauqui saw how the bearded ones and their beasts slowly pulled away the body of his beloved Xochi-pilli. As soon as the men disappeared into the darkness, he ran with all his might toward the village. "The evil ones are taking Xochipilli away! They are stealing the God of Flowers and the Arts!" he shouted from the cobblestone streets.

The young men in the House of Poets rose from their beds. "Who will now inspire us to create our poems?" they asked one another.

"Without our god, who will help us make our music?" the musicians also worried.

"For whom will we dance, if not for Xochipilli?" cried the maidens in the House of Dance.

Among the shadows of the night, the farmers and all the others came together. "Without Xochipilli our crops will be lost," the farmers told one another.

"But how can we fight the evil ones and their fire-spitting weapons?" a man asked.

"Fear not their weapons or their beasts. We shall go after them and bring our Xochipilli back to where he belongs," Itauqui commanded.

"Let us do as the brave Itauqui says," the poets agreed. The musicians and the maidens also joined as Itauqui whirled around and set out down the road. They followed the invaders' footsteps and the tracks of their beasts.

When they reached the end of the road, the men and women spotted the invaders warming themselves around a fire. The tired men rested while Xochipilli's body lay nearby. Itauqui and the others patiently waited.

After the men fell asleep, Itauqui whispered to his friends, "There is no time to waste." They swiftly sneaked through the shadows. Like night ghosts they began to pull with all their might on the ropes still attached to their god. And while the greedy men slept, the worshippers of Xochipilli slowly dragged its body back toward the village. For many hours all pushed and pulled. Their hands blistered and bled from the coarse ropes, but no one grumbled or complained.

Near dawn, when they had come close to the village, Itauqui stopped suddenly. "Listen," he whispered. Everyone stopped and turned to look at him. "I hear the pounding hooves of the beasts."

A young man scampered up a tree and looked down the trail. "They are coming! The bearded ones and their beasts are coming after us!" he warned.

The men and women's voices filled with panic. "How can we save Xochipilli?"

"How can we spare ourselves from the ruthless men?" they asked.

"Hurry!" Itauqui responded. "Help me dig a hiding place for Xochipilli." And quickly all joined him, digging with sharp wooden sticks and scooping out the ground with their bare hands.

After the hole was deep enough, Itauqui again commanded, "Let's now bury our god." The poets, musicians, and dancers helped with their tired arms and bleeding hands until they maneuvered the statue into the hole. While they pushed back the soil to cover its body, the rumble of the beasts' hooves came closer and closer to their ears. Then Itauqui warned, "There is no more time. Go back to the village and save yourselves. Tell the people that our god is safe. Tell all that Xochipilli will never be taken away from our land."

While the men and women ran to the safety of the village, Itauqui stayed behind and finished covering the god with the loose soil. Then he set out on the road, toward the village.

But soon the men appeared. Their angry eyes searched around Itauqui. They rode on their beasts, peeking up the road and into the forest. But the statue of stone had disappeared. The enraged men swarmed around Itauqui and noticed his blistered, bleeding hands. They screamed and yelled at him like maddened animals while their brutal lashes fell mercilessly over his body. But the protector of Xochipilli silently stood still without giving away his secret.

The angered men soon realized that their captive would not tell where the god dressed with jewels lay hidden. Their chief instructed two men and sent them into the forest.

The men returned carrying logs of wood with which they built a fire. After they tied Itauqui's hands, the men placed his feet into the burning embers. But as the hours passed, the pain did not make him speak or beg for mercy. Only the chirping of the birds in the trees and the crackling of the burning coals below his feet broke the silence of the forest. When the pain became too intense to bear, Itauqui finally closed his eyes. He died with a peaceful smile on his face before the eyes of the frustrated men.

The next day after the invaders had gone, the villagers returned to the spot where they had buried Xochipilli. Nearby they found the lifeless body of Itauqui lying on the ground. The men and women wept for him. After unearthing their god, they carried to the village the bodies of both Xochipilli and Itauqui, back where the two belonged.

When the people arrived at the temple, they dug a grave beneath the altar of Xochipilli. After burying Itauqui in it, they finally returned the God of Flowers and the Arts back to his place, above where the loyal Itauqui now rested.

In time, Itauqui became known as the courageous protector of Xochipilli. And his name and courage lived forever in the hearts of the Aztec people.

The Aztecs

The Aztec dynasty began in the year 1376 and flourished in the central valley of México. Their brave warriors, priests, and dancers worshipped the principal god *Huitzilopochtli*, or "Blue Hummingbird on the Left." This deity was represented by the sun, which was worshipped with daily rituals and human sacrifices. The Aztecs called themselves "people of the sun," or "the chosen people."

According to legend, the god *Quetzalcóatl,* or Feathered Serpent, had left on a raft of snakes on the eastern waters. It was said he would return in the year One Reed as a bearded white man. A bright comet that appeared in the sky during the time of Moctezuma the Second was the omen that foretold the coming of the Feathered Serpent.

The Aztec empire came to a sudden end with the arrival of the Spanish conquistadors, headed by Hernán Cortés, in 1519, or the year One Reed according to the Aztec calendar. The emperor Moctezuma the Second believed Cortés to be the long-awaited god who had returned from his exile in the east to reclaim his glory and power. Moctezuma thus instructed his people and warriors not to fight or rebel, but to peacefully surrender to the bearded god and his troops.

Glossary

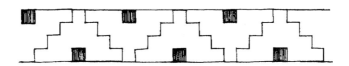

Aríma (ah-ree'-mah) = She who harvests

Atzimba (aht-seem'-bah) = Princess

Balam (bah-lahm') = Sacred jaguar

Curicaveri (koo-ree-kah-vay'-ree) = God of Fire

Huitzilopochtli (weet-see-lo-poacht'-lee) = Blue Hummingbird on the Left, God of War and the Sun

Hunem (ooh-nem') = The hunter

Itauqui (ee-tow'-kee) = The devoted one

Itzá (eet-sah') = Mayan female name

Ixchel (eeks'-chale) = The moon, Goddess of Birth and Medicine

Jade = Green semiprecious stone, highly praised by the Maya

Kupuri (koo-poo'-ree) = Life force

Maize = Corn

Mangrove = Tropical evergreen tree that grows aerial roots

Mara'kame (mah-rah-kah'-may) = Holy man

Mayel (mah-yel') = Chosen one

Moctezuma (moke-tay-soo'-mah) = Angry lord

Nahaci (nah-ah'-see) = Mountain dweller, woman of the forest

Nahuatl (nah-wah'-tul) = Aztec language

One Reed = Aztec year, corresponding to 1519

Quetzal (kate-sahl') = Tropical bird with long tail feathers, native to Central America

Quetzalcóatl (kate-sahl-ko'-ah-tul) = Feathered serpent, God of Life and Learning

Rarámuri (rah-rah'-moo-ree) = Fleet foot, or foot runner

Shaman = High priest

Tahui (tah-oo'-ee) = Great child

Takauyasi (tah-kah-oo-yah'-see) = Father Sun

Tatewari (tah-teh-wah-ree) = Grandfather Fire

Tenochtitlan (teh-noach-teet'-lahn) = Place of the prickly pear cactus, the capital city of the Aztecs

Tepu (tay'-poo) = Three-legged drum

Thicatame (tee-cah-tah'-may) = The leader

Tikal (tee-kahl') = Largest Mayan city of the classic period

Tikámen (tee-kah'-men) = He who speaks

Uru (oo'-roo) = Sacred arrow

Uto-Aztec (oo'-toe az'-tek) = Belonging to the Aztec linguistic family

Wiricuta (wee-ree-koo'-tah) = Sacred desert land, or the center of earth

Xochipilli (so-chee-pee'-yee) = God of Flowers and the Arts

Yumari (yoo-mah'-ree) = Ancient hero

Ziram (see-rahm') = Strong roots

Antonio Hernández Madrigal was born and raised in the state of Michoacán, México, where he often listened to tales told by his great-grandmother, a healer and storyteller of the Tarascan tribe. His is also the coauthor with Tomie DePaola of *Erandi's Braids* and author of *Blanca's Feather*.

Tomie DePaola, best-selling illustrator and winner of the Caldecott Honor Book Award and many other awards, has illustrated nearly two hundred books and has written the stories for nearly one-third of those books. Beloved by children and adults and best known for his Strega Nona character, more than 5 million copies of his books are in print in fifteen different countries.